NOWHERE
NOW HERE

CHARLES SPRINGER

Radial Books

ACKNOWLEDGEMENTS

I would like to thank my editor and publisher, Tricia Yost, for her good humor and unfailing support along with my family and friends, real and imaginary for inspiration in the fashioning of these pieces. Thank you to the editors and staff of the publications in which the following poems have appeared:

Burningword Literary Journal: "Inauguration Day," "Acknowledgments"
Chelsea Station: "Comrades in Arms, Etc."
Corvid Queen, Sword and Kettle Press: "Feat"
Everest Magazine: "Middling"
Forge: "Hand to Hand"
Gertrude: "Captured"
Ghost City Review: "Think"
Gingerbread House: "About Faces"
Leveler: "Toast"
Lindenwood Review: "Work Force"
Pangolin Review: "Sent from Above"
Rabid Oak: "Singing for Supper," "Small Wonder"
Rat's Ass Review: "Phallic Sentiments"
Santa Clara Review: "Not Quite Ripe," "Yellow Ribbon 'Round," "Lend," "Alignments"
Sawbuck: "Patch"
Scarlet Leaf Review: "Funny Weather," "Stuffers," "V for Wings," "Grand Theft"
Sleet: "Calciums," "Chariot of Fire," "Jake's Carnival," "Quake," "Real"
Spank the Carp: "Masters Right Next Door"
Squawk Back: "Day at the Beach"
Stickman Review: "Name Change Game," "Abuzz," "Deliverance"
Street Light: "Check Up or Check Out," "Pine Tale"
Third Wednesday: "At the Last Minute"
Willawaw: "Setting Things Right on a Friday Night"
Zillah: "Dear Envelope,"

*To my mom and dad,
Kathleen and John*

CONTENTS

ONE

I never thought I'd see the day,
said night.

DAY AT THE BEACH

A truck carrying inflated beach balls just skidded off
I-95 near Roanoke and now the beach balls, hundreds,
are dotting the highway causing pileups, quite a few
flying up into trees like giant jelly beans and there's
such a state of joy among the flocks of red-winged
blackbirds and cats are chasing dogs for a change into
the median, dogs that always wanted but never had the
courage to enter and those surviving the chase are re-
lieving themselves like never before and me, I'm just
lying here in the sand listening to the radio, looking at
the sun through my eyelids, waiting for some big new
world to come out of nowhere and bounce off my head.

JAKE'S CARNIVAL

Jake's got to put down stakes right here right now in middle March because we need some truly ripped amusement so I am putting down a fat deposit so Jake can pitch his tents upon the ice and drifts and plow through with his tractor trailers filled with collapsible Ferris wheel and Hurricane and Loop the Loop, and Teacups for the wives and children, into my whiteout pasture and in just two days, move myself and my pale-tone pals into the maddest states of Masquerade and Mayhem, if you know what I mean because we need salvation, salivation of the saltiest kind, we need to shout out dances and dropkick songs until there's nothing left of us but lint and we are good for done!

DELIVERANCE

Thomas is taking the back way into town this morning because there are fewer lights and he's needing fewer lights right now and the traffic ahead of him slows close to a standstill yet keeps moving and in a minute or two most of the cars ahead of him have turned off and he finds himself following this old-fashioned milk cart pulled by a horse whose driver keeps turning around and smiling but Thomas is more interested in getting to where he's going than addressing this historic anomaly which is, by the way, testing his perception of reality not to mention patience and it's gotten really hot out and Thomas's air conditioner is blowing warm so he rolls down his windows to take in some breeze and the cart driver sees him sweating up a little storm and now the collar of his shirt is soaked as they are moseying along and Thomas sees the cart driver is pressing a pint bottle of cold milk to his forehead to cool off so he calls to him, hey you there behind the horse, can you spare one for me and the cart driver says, sorry bud, every bottle I got here is earmarked for delivery to the octo- and nonagenarians in town who pay extra to relive the experience of finding fresh milk on their doorsteps; some say it's like being reborn, a reason to get out of bed in the morning and besides, the cart driver hollers over the rattle of bottles, you won't suffer long there young whippersnapper, look behind you. The iceman cometh.

NEW BATTERIES

Getting fitted for a walk outdoors before lights out, I just knew my new Fido was hankering for a flashlight of his own, so I pulled a little Eveready out of the everything drawer where I kept the collars of his predecessors and thought we were all set to take on the dark but even with my new handheld and his little beacon I'd tied to the top of his head like a miner's lamp, we got lost in the thicket of witch hazel multiplied by its movement of shadows, not to mention our own which were now on the loose way ahead of us but soon enough, me and Fi found ourselves spun around and headed back to the front porch where our shadows were already rocking our rockers.

QUAKE

Moe is hoeing his row of turnips toward a stubborn
clump of quack grass when suddenly the sugar ma-
ples catapult a flock of grackles into a waiting breeze
while the blue sky whites itself out with clouds
and as the sun fades in its effortless dominion, the
ground suddenly does something Moe has no name
for and whatever it is is taking its good ole time and
Moe begins to hop and skip around to surprisingly
keep from falling down while the purple mirror ball
on its pedestal in the backyard thrusts itself into the
carp pond making tiny waves and despite their tiny
size, they team toss the mirror ball at Moe's shiny
head and he catches it even though he's always been
afraid of balls of all kinds and now he sees his face
in it and his newly permanent teeth chatter some
and if he isn't a sight for sore eyes like his father
used to say and when the ground finally stops doing
whatever it was doing and the carp pond calms and
grackles are back on branches, Moe jiggles the mir-
ror ball a little in his hands only to discover right
there in the turnip patch he too can jar a world when
he puts his hoe down.

CAPTURED

I am looking at a picture taken in the eighties of an apartment house on East 79th. A man with a scarf and cap and plaid jacket is crossing the street and appears to be headed for a drug store. The picture appears on page fifty of a book on beginning photography. I post the picture on the web. A week or so later I receive an email from a man claiming to be the one in the picture. His is the only response. Except for the seven from corroborating friends and neighbors. He'd like to meet. Both of us are now in our 60's and neither of us drives in the city. I hop a bus. He rides the subway and we end up in front of the Center for Beginning Photography. He's brought coffee. I've got two pretzels, one with mustard. Suddenly we're surrounded by cameras. We put our arms around each other's shoulders. We crack smiles. After the flashes stop, he pulls pictures from inside his jacket. One's me at the bus stop on my first day in elementary. Another is me on a bicycle. He tells me his mother kept them in a box. A box in the pantry of her kitchen on the 17th floor of an apartment house on the corner of something and East 79th. She'd found them under floorboards in their first house in Scranton. When I ask if she has one of me with a camera, he unfolds a large glossy of a kid in a plaid jacket with a Brownie up to his face. We agree this could really be anybody.

THE VIEW ALONE

Peter pretended to have a sister so his parents would buy her a doll house. He played in it until he was fourteen and it led to his becoming an architect. Peter ended up building this wonderful two-story colonial for his own family of four. The entire back side was constructed of glass panels that slid expensively into side walls. The roof conveniently lifted off so Peter's wife could easily store wedding gifts and holiday decorations at the drop of a hat. There never was nor would there ever be crawl space. The entire house construction was so light Peter's family could pick up and put down just about anywhere on the planet without so much as a hitch. Lately his kids have been itching to go to the moon so Peter's turned everything over to his wife's brother, the astrophysicist in the family to get them there and back, if they'll want to come back. Peter's heard the views are unlike any other and isn't it all about views? Personally, he says he'd like to revolve around a gas giant for a gas giant year or two but that's after the kids are out on their own and he and his wife have gone in totally different directions so it would be just him out in space, him and the view. Then just the view.

SOUNDTRACK

I dial the operator and when she comes on, I tell her I just had a really good breakfast, pancakes and sausages, and she says she skipped breakfast and then I say I have a doctor's appointment later this morning and the news may not be good but then it could be great and I might want to buy that new pickup I've been passing on the lot every morning and purposely run over the neighbor kid's bicycle blocking the sidewalk and that I'd like on this, what might just turn out to be my very last day on earth to locate a last-day-on-earth composer, someone like Oscar-winner John Williams or even Oscar-winner John Williams himself to write me a soundtrack because I want my last day to have a soundtrack and the operator puts me on hold for a few seconds and comes back with a number to call and I ask if she'd like a copy when it's released and she says she doesn't listen to any music but on-hold music but thanks anyway and I never did get around to calling John Williams or someone like him.

What a picture! Mike, out the kitchen window at his easel in his Speedo, painting his backyard in his backyard! I can see him from the bathroom window, bedroom window too. How he fractions himself like that I can't take in so I go out there and ask him. That's why the triptych, he explains. You got tickets for your trip? I ask reluctantly with a frown. Hard to hear out here with all the noises, birds and dogs and cats, garbage truck down the alley. You hear birds and dogs and cats, garbage truck down the alley? he asks back. By now I'm standing right up next to him and what I see so far looks nothing like backyard. Oh, there's trees and shrubs and seas of grass but one of the panels has a beautiful blue pool painted near its bottom. There is no pool in Mike's backyard. My last yard had a pool, he says, and I've been pining for it so I've put it in the picture. The water looks so real; can we jump in? I ask, and Mike chuckles, says, give me five, and in just those many strokes, he's got us floating on our backs on rubber rafts with built-in holders for our beer cups. Then, without asking, he paints us soaring high above the sugar maples, gliding in a cloudless sky. I confess to him, I knew you had it in you. Hey, can that be Leo waving from your vanishing point? I ask. If you want it to be Leo, Mike says, I'll make it Leo. What he's been up to anyways these days? I ask. When did his Lisa put on that smile?

NEAR SO FAR

Phil lives in a little house in the country. The house is surrounded by a full representation (in English and Latin) of trees. On the ground grows a crazy quilt of fern and moss and uncultivated floral arrangements. Up in the air flies the usual pantheon of local birds and butterflies and uncared-about bugs. Phil decides one afternoon to leave his little house and spiral out into its curiously confusing surroundings. If one were to map the twists and turns he took, the result would compare to the internal arrangement of human intestines, or better yet, the frenetic state of an Uncle Wiggily game board. Phil finds himself as always, for this is not his first nor will it be his last outing, at the pond. We'd thought about the ocean but that's too big for anyone to find himself at. The pond then.

WAR EFFORTS

Me and Joe are out hoeing potatoes when he reminds
me the submarine is reemerging down at the pier this
afternoon. Wanna go, he asks? Will be too hot to hoe.

I remind him of what happened last time. You know
how those skinny navy boys like the real thing. All
they get underwater is reconstituted.

Well what about your chickens? Joe asks. You know
how much those skinny navy boys like chasing chick-
ens?

I've got my chickens covered, I tell him. At the snap
of fingers they all hop into their rabid fox disguis-
es. They're enough to scare anybody, especially now
they've learned how to stagger across the chicken
yard and foam at the mouth.

We're forgetting, Joe says, those skinny navy boys are
our fighting boys. They keep our nation safe from all
the isms, especially hypnotism. I don't ever want to
be seen cackling on a stage somewhere and flapping
these flimsy arms, bobbing my head for cracked corn.
Besides, these boys deserve a real meal.

You're right Joe. You bring the spuds. I'll bring wings.
We'll get the wives to dance with them after dessert!
Hell, I'll dance with them myself, Joe says. It's been a
while since I did the mashed potato.

WORKFORCE

I phone the electric company, tell its customer service representative my lights have been flickering on and off for hours. Not to mention the havoc the power's been playing with the radio and the ceiling fans. The customer service representative tells me I need to call an electrician. You don't know about these things? I ask unblinkingly. I know next to nothing about wires and switches and currents, he admits, in fact, nobody here in twenty-two cubicles knows about wires and switches and currents. We only know about customer service. So I ask, in those moments the power blinks off, I won't be charged? In your dreams, he says, in your dreams. Are you in my dreams? I ask. Of course, he says flatly, wherever you are, we are. That's what makes us number one in the region, the nation. Tomorrow, the world.

TWO

While breathing deeply lately,
Sarah has uncovered old smells.

TOAST

I pop up on the wrong side of bed. Right side faces the window. It's very dark out. I easily slam into the wall. I feel my way for what seems the width of the room. It's really its length. I meet up with another wall. I'm in a corner. I've been in a corner before but not without cause. I about-face, see the whole room all at once. It's really very nice-sized. In fact, there's room for a fridge and a stove. A professional four-slice toaster on an island. Then you pop up on the right side. I reach out to you. We meet and greet beneath the skylight. We tilt back our heads. There the two are, one atop the other, the sun and the moon like marmalade and margarine on this crispest morning of all mornings.

NOWHERE NOW HERE

Four fellow New Yorkers assure me over the back of
their booth that the middle of nowhere is in Alabama
and easily gotten to by car. Assuming they have been
there, I ask how was it, nowhere's middle and all?
They admit in unison they never left the East Side
but to visit the Botanical Gardens. By no means do
I let a simple question lead to expanded conversa-
tion which then has us in some gallery in Chelsea or
strolling high on the High Line. I just want to know
if even the near reaches of nowhere are worth a trip
around the block. Their laughter runs the gamut from
tee-heeing to guffawing. I realize I either have splots
of eggs benedict on my face or I am indeed headed
somewhere. Which is what I left my apartment for in
the first place. I am finally able to get them to draw
breaths when I reveal that nowhere, if you have been
there or not, can also be now here. I also tell them
I occupy an entire floor at the Pierre just to make
them tear a little in their bouillabaisse for which they
thank me because they say it definitely needed some
salt. I reply on my way out that everywhere one goes
these days, there seems less and less. I then grab a
cab that takes me south off the meter.

THINK

When Sara goes outside she doesn't get wet. But it's pouring out and she has neither slicker nor umbrella. If you look really close, you'll see the droplets deflect not even an inch from her skin. I think she thinks the rain away and since thoughts have been declared things by the thinking community, they can come between what's wet and what's dry and stays dry. Personally I like to think as little as possible and stay indoors as much as possible. It's not Sara's life but it's a good one.

CHIP OFF THE BLOCK

Chip has been standing in front of that door for maybe an hour. He still hasn't knocked. Nor has he tried the knob. I know because I have good ears like everyone else here on Fifteen. No one on Fifteen has bad ears. Chip's aunt and uncle live in D and Chip stops by once a week to check up on them. Usually on Tuesday but sometimes a Friday. In the morning but not always.

Two weeks ago Chip stood in front of the door for so long he started to lose weight. I watched through my peephole. Mrs. Weaver down the hall brought him one of her oatmeal bars and an orange. Chip woofed down the bar but pocketed the tangerine; it was a tangerine, not an orange. He'd hold onto it for when he got out on the street. Sticky fingers went everywhere there.

We all thought, including the superintendent, that Chip couldn't handle the disappointment if no one was home. Or maybe he feared getting germs by touching the hardware. Everyone agreed he most likely couldn't be trusted with keys.

Truth was, we found out from Chip himself, he never opened a door in his life. He either passed through where there was none or snuck in behind someone else. For Chip, the revolving and the automatics were godsends. Only way he'd open a door himself, he once told me, is if he got tips like his Uncle Buster.

Little blue box some tacks came in is not moving by itself. I hear a faint repeating ring like a work bell near the baseboard. On my belly, head in my hands, I see four ants the irresistible hue of construction workers in late August. I watch them from half to a larger pie slice of an hour move the little blue tack box toward a plastic amber pill bottle stuck in the middle of an ice cream spill even older.

One by one a cast of little character ants methodically carries seed resembling amaranth and toll-house cookie crumbs I'd know anywhere to the top of the amber pill bottle and drops them in. Meanwhile the little blue tack box arrives and is slid into position next to the pill bottle. One singularly leggy ant jumps up and down on a stowaway tack to hold the box in its place.

A bell clangs heartily, unmistakably the dinner bell and all goes dark. Except there is this glowing inside a Tic-Tac box in a grove of dust bunnies within ant-walking distance of the little blue tack box. And in the Tic-Tac's glowing center, a spark I have to get down on my hands and knees to see and all I see is wonder and the ants do too.

ALL THE WAY

Ada asks what the matter was and Abe, aka Mr. Fix-it, or who some call Mr. FlubItUpSomeMore, says it was ajar. Ada asks the age-old question, how could it be a jar when it's a door? Abe, accustomed to doing the occasional odd job for the befuddled, tries to explain but Ada keeps right on complaining about the sagging center of her marble cake. Ever the rescuer, Abe tells Ada he'll eat the center, he hates crusty edges and always says no to corner pieces even when starved. Ada's so happy, she accompanies his selection with a tumbler of whole milk. Abe is sated. Ada settles up with a crisp fifty from her panda cookie jar, she collects everything panda, and Abe tells her next time the door doesn't close all the way to call a professional who knows all the angles. He can't resist telling her too how he just adores anything panda and Ada gets suspicious, thinks Abe might want something more. The pair ends up flailing their arms at each other when suddenly the door slams shut on its own and remains so for hours.

SENT FROM ABOVE

Right after my half-brother broke it off with his
motorcycle mama, a crow appeared outside on the
window sill and would not leave, even when my
half-brother knocked on the glass with the tip of
his shotgun barrel. Even when he raised the sash
and swung the barrel around in the crow's shiny
face, it would not leave its perch. Seeing this as a
real pickle, my half-brother grabbed his keys off the
cupboard and decided to go for a ride and when he
approached his bike, the crow was claw-fisted to its
handlebars. My half-brother thought as soon as he
starts up the engine and revs it a little, the crow will
take off. It did, but then promptly returned to fill in
the deep depression left on the seat behind him. No
matter how fast my half-brother rode or how sharp
he leaned into curves, the crow was right there be-
hind him, crowing away.

NOT QUITE RIPE

Myrtle's in the fruit section sorting melons, canta-
loupes mostly, mid-February when she finds a warm
one with a power cord attached to where its stem
used to be but nowhere on the cord's a switch, just
a plug on the end for the receptacle and now she
thumps the cantaloupe, sounds right, then sniffs it,
smells ripe and so she tosses it in her cart and I can
tell by the quickness in her step, you see I'm right be-
hind her, fingering grapes, she can't wait to get this
baby home and plug it in and I cannot wait either so
now we're in her kitchen where she plugs it in: noth-
ing, not a thing, no lighting up, no ballooning up, no
hum, no toasty crackle of little white seeds inside,
oh, for a moment back in the store Myrtle thought
this melon might be a novelty clock radio like her
lobster telephone and elephant refrigerator but no,
so she gets a knife to cut it up and after each smooth
stroke, the blade gets sharper, a sharpness you can
see with your naked eye and when the knife begins
to cut all by itself, she pulls the plug and the knife
goes back into its block and Myrtle, Myrtle has gone
off cantaloupes at least until they're in season.

DOMESTICITY

I've been spying on my neighbor all morning. His dog, actually. Damn thing's been barking from window to window to window. After a few minutes, it got ahead of me. When I finally caught up, I swear it stuck its tongue out. I ended up throwing a rock and not only busted the glass but knocked the dog out as well. I ran to the opening and reached in, careful not to get cut on the shards, and pulled a dog mask off my neighbor's face. Gee gods, Bart, you okay, you want me to call the vet? Not funny, he says, and what's with that pussycat mask? Oh this, it's the only way my wife will feed me and let me curl up in her bed. Got it, Bart says, having me as the house dog is the only way my wife feels safe and not carry that damn pistol around in her apron. Hey Bart, I say, let's put on our masks and scamper down to the pound. We'll show them life on the outside's all it's cracked up to be.

SCRIBE

I should have written it down.

What? asks the multi-thousand year old scribe.

The phone number. It's ten digits long and my brain only has room for five at a time. I'm a wiz though when it comes to zip codes. Want to know one for Ashtabula, Ohio? For Dubuque?

Nah, that's okay. But thanks for asking.

Hungry? I've got, let's see, exactly forty-five cents here in my pocket. We could split fish and chips. Better yet, we could keep the forty-five cents and fish for some chips in that barrel over there. The one by the pond. If not that one, then some other. There are thousands all over the city. Be glad to go around with you if you've got the time and determination.

Oh, I've got the time. And I was born with determination. Not something I just picked up willy-nilly.

Like those two extra toes? People'd pay good money to see those little piggies in action. Try sticking a felt tip between them and get them scribing as well. Maybe even toy with some manuscript illumination.

Hmm, never gave it a thought.

Don't worry about it. You don't have to think. That's what's so wonderful. That, and your ability to sit still for years at a time.

REPEAT ORDER

I tell friends Ray and Dale about my farm. Of course they want to come and see it. Yes, with pigs and cows and chickens and even a couple goats. Most of all they want to see the horses.

Last years' unfortunately are cracked and peeling and don't hold air. Where's that receipt? Ah, yes, Bobby's Farmyard Creations. Let's see, 6 horses at $200 per - 3 roans, 1 pinto, 2 mules—all in "pasture-grazing" positions. I call Bobby up and he says he can repeat my order for the same money and ship overnight. Deal!

Ray and Dale arrive early. We spend time in the barn (Ray loves cows and Dale is a bit of a pig himself) and then head out to the paddock to see the horses. Ray and Dale comment none of them ever seems to look up, doesn't even startle at a whistle. I say it must be the new crop of grass. Fortunately Ray and Dale know exactly what I mean and fortunately neither one of them rides.

We walk back to the house for a nice brunch on the side porch (these guys can put it away!) and then I drive them to the station. Just as they're about to board, we look up. The pinto and both mules are floating beneath a little thunderbumper! I explain to Ray and Dale they enjoyed your visit so much they've just come to see you off. Ray and Dale are so overcome with emotion, they themselves deflate right there on the platform. I pick them up, put them on the train and head home.

Not surprisingly the pinto and mules are back in
the paddock with the roans. How thoughtful of the
roans to wait so they could all fall apart together.
Oh, almost forgot to mention the sheep dog, bonus
gift with every repeat order. Him I keep fully inflated
at all times on the rug in front of the fake fire.

THREE

*Sam always thought a sinkhole
was where he poured the Drano
until the Drano plant disappeared.*

NAKED AND AFRAID

A man and a woman each brings to an episode one item like a machete or a pot to boil water in. No food, no clothes, no toilet paper. They're dropped off out of a Jeep or pickup or boat in some jungle or desert or swamp and have to survive for twenty-one days. They suffer hunger, dehydration, mosquitoes, fire ants, the deadliest snakes, wild boars, wild camels, extreme heat, extreme cold, typhoons, avalanches, the ugliest bats in the bat kingdom, tropical and non-tropical depression. They sleep in some rickety shelter they try to hold together with spit. Oh, just in case you're wondering, their private parts are blurred by the TV show's producers. This week the stars are Jesse and Tonya. One, plump, one, a former marathoner, one, a cupcake baker, one, a door-to-door salesperson, one from the Bronx, one from Pocatello. It's a match made in reality hell and I've come to love TV broadcasting hells: Jesse and Tonya shaking their multi-functional coconut shells at us and each other and what that could be under their fingernails is as close to naked and afraid as I want to get sitting here in my thirty-year-old naugahyde recliner in my fourth-day plaid boxers, devouring a tub of caramel walnut fudge with no spoon.

REAL

Randy rings up the circus in town and tells the young lady on the other end he can disappear at the drop of a hat and do you have any openings? She says to come on over and fill out an application. Randy informs her he has a tough time sometimes holding onto a pencil and she says, no problem, she'll lend him a hand. When he gets there, she tells him she can't see him and to stop fooling around. Randy tells her, put on your glasses and she says, oh yeh, right, silly me. Half an hour goes by and she hands him his costume. This is the fat lady's costume, he says, how's about a nice tie and tails? I'm sorry, she says, those are reserved for the ringmaster. Only the ringmaster gets to wear tie and tails. Well then, what about a crisp top hat and cane? Only if you can take the white rabbit and doves and clothesline of multi-colored handkerchiefs with you when you disappear, she says. Now look here, Randy says, I'm not a magician. What I do is real. Oh, that, she says, yes, well, perhaps you'd better keep looking.

FAMOUS ROOF

A song has sung down off my roof, one leg out, one leg in my window and I have to wait for both legs in before I name it. I certainly don't have to tell you it's one you've known forever but not liked all that much. I yell up to the roofers through the ceiling, I don't hear nails going into shingles let's hear nails going into shingles. I yell again, sounds more like tapping, are you dancing around up there? I finally shuffle into my shoes, go outside, look up, get dizzy and no one's up there, no elves, nothing, not even walnuts falling off the walnut tree, no birds of any consequence, no left-on generator for the tarred-up radio, no radioactive sleet. Just who remains of the Solid Gold Dancers and some backup singers from the 70's who lived here once while waiting for big breaks.

PINE TALE

Henry slept on the hardwood floor last night with his left, then right ear to it and both heard the same things that the floor was remembering about its early years in what was once the local national forest and was wondering, pining away actually for its fellow timbers and what had become of them, what might they have turned into and had they been turned on a lathe or sliced into veneer or cut into pre-cuts for table and chair parts or prostheses even or pile upon pile of what were to become Dixon Ticonderoga pencils for scribbling pupils or maybe ground up from the ground up into chips to glue back together to make wallboard or chips for around the bases of trees shading big fancy brick houses and all this had led Henry to tears, so many the floor was starting to warp and curl up around him like a boat which would float Henry out of there should the water pipes burst from oh so much pressure but then too the floor could be, uh-oh for Henry, turning into a box.

PICKED UP

I was flying down the road when this trooper flicked his lights and cranked his siren. I immediately pulled over. After tapping my bumper just a little, he got out of his cruiser and walked up to my window, already rolled down of course, and tipped his cap. Please step out of the vehicle and walk the line, he instructed. I walked the line as straight as if I'd painted it myself, which I just happened to have done a week ago today. Why the swerving? he asks. I told him there were all these turtles, at least a dozen of them on the pavement, none in a hurry to get across. I see, he said, but he didn't see a one. Next time, he said, just run 'em over! Far too many in the commonwealth as it is and by the way, here's a ticket. It's to our annual ball. I took it, then he took my arm, escorting me back to my pickup, telling me on the way how he really dug my alligator shoes and was looking forward to a dance.

SEED OF FORTUNE

Drake's in the grapes aisle at the fancy fruit store. He never knew grapes to come in so many sizes and colors. He pulls off a fat one, pops it in his mouth, never thinking of how many other fingers have fingered it or noses sneezed on it, never thinking of his petty bite as theft and within seconds its one seed begins to unravel in his mouth and when he spits it into his hand, it resembles a fortune from a take-out cookie and he's all excited because he thinks he's about to get some big news from afar, sage words to inspire him, maybe even make him believe in a higher power so he rolls the message out on his palm where it reads, Yo, spitwad, it's Ho Jo, the guy from fifth grade whose eye you almost put out. I'm waiting for you outside behind your Isuzu. You'd better show, straw breath.

ABOUT FACES

Ted and Alice keep a closet full of faces. They hang on little hangers next to shirts and trousers and skirts and blouses. The arrangement makes getting ready for work easier. Shoes point out the door and neither Ted nor Alice worry about underwear.

Ted is big on linen. Alice goes for blends of poly and cotton. Silk or satin for evening. In Macy's Facewear, Ted selects his favorite loose fitting with snaps behind the ears. Alice likes her faces nice and tight over her perfect, high cheekbones and with hidden zippers. Ted sports medium tan summer and winter. Occasionally camouflage in fall. Alice delights in bone white with subtle blush touches on her nose tip and along her perfect, high cheekbones.

Ted lets his boxer wear his face on occasion. same with Alice and her schnoodle. They usually only do this when the famous dog photographer has been spotted with his camera down at the gazebo. Spoilers that they are, Ted and Alice went out last Saturday and got Rocky and Trixie faces of their own to wear.

One morning in a hurry dressing in the dark, Ted and Alice accidentally put the other's face on. It was bound to happen sooner or later. Ted's pool boy Rusty waved and winked as Ted was backing out of the driveway. Neighbor Abby caught Alice's eye and wiggled and winked from her rose bed. No one gave a second thought to why Ted and Alice switched cars. Just then each of them caught glimpses of his and her selves in the rearview. Whole neighborhood heard the squeals of u-turns at the ends of the boulevard.

When Ted and Alice saw themselves as each other, it
happened. They fell in love all over. During a cocktail
lunch they toyed with the idea of gender reassign-
ments but decided to stick with what they knew. Af-
ter steaming apple pie and dollops of whipped cream,
Alice held the ladder while Ted screwed a new bulb in
the closet socket.

HOVER

After what had seemed an endless adolescence, Alan picked himself up off his folding chair and asked the fan to dance. He held it at a safe and proper distance as recommended in the manual. The fan and Alan spun round and round until the electric was all used up and the band put down its instruments. Alan walked the fan back to his room, propped it in the window. Before he had a chance to plug it in, a night breeze sucked it out. The fan hummed like a hummingbird as it coursed over the poplars. Blades slowed and sped alternately on their plastic axle. As it headed toward a major star cluster, Alan reached for his trusty baton and twirled it over his head. For the first time in a long time he was able to hover and at this reporting, refuses to set down.

INAUGURATION DAY

Wife calls me from her cell, says all the way to work whitetails lined the roadway, four and five deep in places, says they looked like passengers behind the line to board a train. I remind her that today's the day the governor comes to town with his entourage and motorcade. I ask her if she saw the rabbits. Come to think of it, she says, it did look like the doe were wearing fuzzy slippers. And were there birds perched atop bucks' antlers? Hundreds, maybe thousands, in the voice she gathers for amazement. She asks if they've all left their nests to greet the governor as he passes. I tell her each and every creature have been summoned for extinction. Did you not see the front end loaders, dump trucks in the background? Silly me, she says, you're right, always with a new administration.

FOUR

*I can count on one hand
any number of times.*

Dick found a future in used cars as had his Uncle Fred, whom by the way, Dick liked more than his father. Fortunately Dick never found the words to tell him so but did convince me SUVs were just around the corner so get one now. Dick married Helen who brought along her son and daughter and cat and dog from a previous union.

Jane grew up of course and in her twenties did a stint as a pole dancer in that joint next to the Super 8. She saved her money, went back to school and became an optician, in addition to becoming the best little wife any chief of police could ask for. Last time she dilated my pupils, there were no children.

Sally came out in the 10th grade and promptly came between the phys. ed. teacher and Miss Martine, that's with an e, who taught French. Sally soon quit school and moved to the bay area where after a succession of trysts, she's living alone with her fifth cat named Puff. Word is she's looking.

And Spot? Spot ran. He ran into the yard. He ran into the park. He'd still be running but he ran into the street. I ran over him with my brand new SUV. He's now in doggone heaven where he's running in the White House.

HAND TO HAND

My right hand is writing a letter to the hand it held last
night at the showing of *My Left Foot*.

My right arm is stretched to the limit not quite three
feet counting the distance from my shoulder to a felt
tip where it articulates Dear Someone or Other.

As the writing is small, a six on a font scale, and my
eyes cannot read aloud, the fold of my brain that re-
cords flitters and flutters records my hand's heart as it
spills and spells out its guts.

My brain cannot speak at all and my mouth must not
have been doing its part or my right hand wouldn't be
writing to some hand it has more than just touched.
My mouth must have had its tongue in an ear when
nothings weren't enough.

My mouth deservedly got slapped by a hand out of no-
where and is shut, grounded for one month, and two
times a day my left hand washes it out with soap and
talks to it like a puppet, telling it not what my right
hand has written thus far but the "sorry" an ear likes
to hear.

My mouth always wanted its own ear to stick its tongue
into. My ear always wanted its own acoustic guitar and
amp and ten fingers.

Here, near the bottom, the one line one eye can make
out says my right hand wants to "squeeze you until you
drop off, watch you walk on two fingers, tackle Ravel's
Concerto for the Left Hand on the spinet!"

MIDDLING

8 a.m., and after a medium breakfast of Lipton tea and mixed berry jelly toast, Todd jaywalks to the middle of the road. He's been to the middle many times before but only for seconds while crossing. This time could turn into something really perpendicular.

It all goes pretty smoothly down the—look out for the pothole!–double yellows. Almost as if they are made for his feet and the stride of his miler legs. Drivers whizzing by flip him the bird and simultaneously allow ample berth but he still catches cinder spray off the shoulders. Road kill is minimal. Two crows bob at a puddle.

Todd enters a passing zone where a lot of broad jumping is required so he's brought along his pogo stick from the hall closet. This isn't coincidence; Todd always looks forward. Sooner than expected he reaches town's outskirts.

Road's middle here is pure sod. Clover, with a sprinkling of ground berry and arbutus. Hard not to look down when he walks, he occasionally loses his balance. Natural beauty does that to Todd. He hates when he tramples, so he straddles, and from behind, looks like he's rode in on a horse. Fortunately a café pops up up ahead and fortunately it's noon.

Todd is anticipating the café's buffet. Middling makes a belly rumble. Just so happens the couple in Booth 7 saw Todd on the danger curve a little before eleven and are happy to see him in one piece. They spring for his soup, salad and two entrees. This is the turnaround he's been waiting for.

Right after the bread pudding, or maybe custard this
time, Todd makes a beeline over to the police acad-
emy. In no time at all he's town's director of traffic,
with white gloves and whistle, the whole shebang,
gesticulating at rush hour in the intersection.

CHARIOT OF FIRE

It was a pleasantly cool spring evening and neigh-
bors in the hood were champing at the bit to be
outside on their flagstone patios. Next door, Ben-
ny, a retired perpetrator by profession, was not one
to pass up an opportunity to stun and so began to
spread the flames of evening warmth and crackle
with his wheelbarrow. He ranked split logs inside its
tub, spritzed some lighter fluid, struck a match on
his cheek stubble and poof! In less than no time he'd
lit the pits in backyards up and down the block. In no
time a "burn out back" had become a pleasantly cool
spring evening institution. Expectedly it spread to
other streets and towns and provinces where prov-
inces were still governances and just like water and
earth and air, fire returned to spectacle with Benny,
its self-appointed charioteer. From then on, every
time we saw him wheeling down the alley, we raised
our tiki-torches and shouted Here, here, a little fire
if you please, over here!

AMERICAN PARKED CAR

I'm in this beautiful parking lot. It's a small city lot perimetered with trees and of course, meters. So wonderful in the summer when the leaves are up but in the winter when the leaves are down, cars, even pickups get lost.

It is my car I do not see while the leaves are on. I've looked everywhere. Oh, Miss Metermaid, a moment please, have you seen the red and white two-door of my dreams with the western sky blue interior?

CHECK UP OR CHECK OUT

Friday is library day for Ray who picked Friday because it kinda rhymes with library and other days don't so much and becoming well-read and new worldly is high up on the list in Ray's lunch pail. Anyway Ray arrives and says hello to the girl at the desk and beelines over to periodicals where he selects an issue of *People* and in no time remembers having read this very issue last year, the issue about Brad and his sorrowful breakup and as Ray gets up to make another selection, hopefully one where Brad's back in love, the girl from the desk is beckoning to Ray and telling him, the doctor will see you now, and Ray being a little tired and depressed since Brad's breakup, figures how could it hurt and follows.

LEAP OF FAITH

First and last time I leapt off the ironing board had to have been pre-permanent press. I think I was nearing twelve. Didn't break any bones but bled from the chin and felt like the roof of my mouth was stuck to the living room ceiling. For nearly a week I spoke only when spoken to. I admit now I took pride in catapulting the ironing board through our big picture window and costing me a year's allowance. No new LPs, no more accessories for my ten-speed, no beach and all summer long, I literally went the extra yards to cover the cost of a new window's installation. When winter came, everyone was grateful for the best in double glaze. We could sit close and see clear and not shiver as snow came down upon lawns I'd intimately come to know like my mother's pressed sheets. I forgot to mention the new ironing board I bought for her and how forgiveness too has its price and can be paid over time.

CALCIUMS

I saw that very tusk, the one pictured in the paper, over at the Dairy Queen two nights ago. I kicked at it a little to see if it was real. Where I'd kicked it turned to powder; my big toe bore a slight bruise. The tusk was rhino-esque, not elephantine. It gave off an odor not unlike ox. On closer examination I think it was the root part of Dr. Hodges' Happy Tooth. He'd reported it missing to the police who reported it in the paper. Dr. Hodges loved Happy Tooth. He took it home everyday from its pedestal in Reception. When taking his two kids to school, it rode in the backseat, buckled in between them and for awhile there, whole town thought he and the Mrs. had adopted. Anyhow, the tusk was carefully removed to the Dairy Queen Museum in middle Wisconsin. After months of restoration, it ranked right up there in visitor attendance with the museum's biggest hole in cheese. What a match they'd become, not unlike Dr. and Mrs. Hodges.

PATCH

Just outside Leftover's Diner, Patch sits shaking on the bench, waiting for his next set of instructions in front of the newspaper box and whether they will come complete on fronts of T-shirts going by or as single sweater letters, he has to spend a morning puzzling but most of the time he looks like he's just waiting for the bus that never comes and so I buy him tea he stirs with his pencil when he isn't writing diner menus which people line up to see just how beautiful eggs over easy with sausages can read but then last Saturday the waitress had to speak the specials while the box outside sat empty with its door left open and the bench was gone and the air, the air had a fickle glow from the blinking yellow light and some folks walking by like extras said they saw Patch down at the ocean fishing in a bottle.

GUNSCHMOKE

Newly took the Ford when he left Plymouth about four in the morning and arrived at the Chrysler Building before daybreak where he spit on his cuff and brought a nice shine to its doorknob, ran the toll at the tunnel on his way to Dodge to sup burnt coffee and tinned beans with Festus who'd already hunched down with Matt and Dillon, all three, cardboard cut-outs, Newly didn't ask, just thrilled to be in their company and the lights, the cameras, the lame horses and nobody's dogs, out-of-range buffalo, scoop and bucket guys, a honky-tonk piano named Sam with nicotine nails, gunplay and plenty of it fired into the hearts and ceilings of pasteboard scenery, a US Marshall with a badge named Kitty who supported garters and high hair and leaked of sarsaparilla all Saturday night into Sunday meeting where Jesus himself looked hand-drawn on the wanted poster.

ACKNOWLEDGMENTS

First Friday, and I am only visually deconstructing a mixed medium while sipping a snappy little chardonnay and blowing foam through my minced bologna when I trip over my own two feet and slice a piece of thigh on the slivers, squirt blood floor to ceiling on a new white wall and spectators gather while I text for an Uber to Urgent Care to get stitched up, then return to where everyone surrounds me like iron filings on a north magnetic pole, not out of concern for my accident but in awe of it although Pollock would deny the accident and I am gracious and even a bit proud yet properly acknowledge the on-call physician's assistant, the glassblower, the grape stomper, the casing stuffer skyping from a range of locations and of course, my parents in assisted living for their feet in this.

SINGING FOR SUPPER

How far we gotta go yet, I ask, and Mom says about
a hundred mules and in no time we're there at East
Meats West Steakhouse where I've already decided
on surf 'n turf with three glops of frozen custard af-
ter and there have to be at least sixty seventy mules
tied up outside, some to fence rails, some to the big
light pole in the parking lot that looks like a broken
down carousel and some mules, not tied up at all
who just wander, two out onto the roadway where
one got clobbered and is being snuck in through East
Meats West Steakhouse's back kitchen door, cancel
the turf, and all that braying, it's begun to attract
the attention of the town choir filling up inside but
who are now staggering out and harmonizing unlike
anything I've ever heard, bit barbershop, not quite
tabernacle, still heavenly-inspired like what must
have raised up out of the ark after the water went
down and it looks like everyone at East Meats West
Steakhouse is taking a mule home, no mule would be
without one and no home would be home without a
mule and many got to go along to church, some even
got baptized and those with good ears got to bray
in the Christmas story pageant and occasionally on
street corners with bongos and guitars and the pace
of life in Stubbornville, Ohio has picked up quite a
bit and the only things out of tune now are the flies.

SANDWICH

While making a sandwich for my pop conked out on
the sofa, I couldn't remember if he liked his mayo
well inside or spread to the edges or slopping over
them and I knew he didn't want to be kept waiting
so I only slopped mayo over two edges and left two
edges brown and crusty, these he could back into his
palm and I called to him when the table was set and
watched as he sat licking all the edges with his tongue
as if I could do nothing right or no wrong at all.

ORAL HYGIENE

My father took me with him to the only bookstore
in a hundred miles to buy a DIY how-to on livestock
dentistry and while there I heard and saw but under-
stood nothing the man behind the podium read he'd
written in his skinny book of verse anyone could take
home for a mere six bucks and my father told me,
save your money for a rainy day, just happened to be
the following Sunday when my mother yanked me off
to church first time in galoshes, I'd just turned seven,
where a man in robes read from a book so fat he did-
n't even try to pick it up and cradle it, words I'd never
heard before, words I'd wanted to say myself, even
own, so when a plate of money got passed around, I
dropped what I had saved onto it and later took his
book, not all that heavy really, more like a ham, but
at the door while shaking my mother's hand, the man
in robes made me put the big book back, would not
give back my dollars on that plate, called me a fibber
and I called him a faker, the first of many f words my
mother failed to wash out of my mouth.

NEW STATE

By executive order the country just added a new state
to its union and as you might expect, flocks are al-
ready filling it up, flocks of turkeys, flocks of sheep,
flocks of thoughts that think they've died and gone
to heaven knows where the boundaries are and in
this state still to be named and capitalized, chief ex-
ports exported, flags hoisted, there will be balance,
an equality of ilk, new governor appointed likes that
word, intends to use it in all his speeches, private as
well as public and what's most promising and brow
furrowing at the same time is this new state's per-
fect climate and the fact that every other month the
clocks will stop for everyday to become Saturday and
yes, my fellow outsiders, there will be a wall, a wall
of projectile-proof plastic our leader says he'll make
perfectly clear, a clarity he claims only he and his
saved will see through.

TED'S

I own a mule and am moving to a new apartment that doesn't allow pets so I explained to the manager Ted's a working mule, he'll push and pull for you, he'll kick and shove and even wake you up in the morning if you want and the manager informs me Ted's a goat, can you imagine my shock, and goats are allowed on the premises at no extra charge and I tell the manager I so had my heart set on Ted's being a mule and pay-ing his own way and the manager says, okay, but no monkey business.

POT LUCK

Jim pries open a can of beans with his Bowie knife
and licks its edge with his tongue that's never known
the taste of blood or beans but blood and beans taste
like the best barbeque between buns from town's
baker who's Jim's brother-in-law from his fourth
marriage of inconvenience lasting merely months of
hellish high water too much per minute every minute
of days into nights and up again at six for a coffee fix
lasting seconds, all his third hand could tick off 'til
Jim's boss got ticked off and fired him on the spot at
the start of the way out, out of work, out of power, out
of his Thanksgiving gourd, so somebody write a note
to who's bringing gourds and tell them bring extras
because Jim is as knife happy as he was a pint ago or
ever.

FIVE

*John's sense of wonder became heightened
at the Museum of Ordinary Things.*

DIMENSIONS

Have you ever seen a bowl so big it makes the room
it sets in look small? And so you measure the room
and it is small but it makes no excuses or apologies
until one night the bowl hairlines itself against the
back wall and lets out a yelp that wakes up the dog
who's been sleeping on the roof ever since the bowl
rolled into his little house and of course the owner
of the little house, the dog and the bowl is himself
asleep in a hammock between the twin elms because
the Chia pet his boss gave him for Christmas has
taken over every room of his little cookie cutter;
it's like a jungle in there, he exclaims every time
he wakes up, then goes back to sleep dreaming the
same-sized dream as his dog.

STUFFERS

Last year Herman found real human feet cut off just above the ankles in his Christmas stockings tacked to the mantle and found them to be surprisingly happy feet with wiggly toes eager to tickle the ivories and arches hard as marble with the most perfect curves and Herman kept these stocking stuffers active with polonaises on the piano and poses of ancient architectural passages and had made himself and all of his feet a family but only Herman's own feet danced, only Herman's own feet skipped and kicked balls and mean dogs until they wore out and he became bound to a wheelchair while his stocking stuffer feet had become too high and mighty to get their bottoms dirty pushing him around so Herman knocked them down a peg or two with his arm extender and ran them over, forward and reverse, forward and reverse, Herman ground them into the carpet where they became part of the pile.

DID YOU ORDER THIS?

Me and my buddy whose ears don't work go to the bookstore and there is this guy there reading what he wrote, risky poems they sounded like to me and after the reading, my buddy who can lip read shares his impressions and it sounds as though my buddy and I have been listening to two different people because what my buddy read on the reader's lips in no way jived with what I heard with my two good ears and my buddy and I go in together for the reader's book but none of the writings are what we remembered and now my buddy and I are hungry because readings always leave you hungry so we head for some burgers and fries where going through the drive-through, we hear and see the very same poet-reader taking and making our order too salty and not salty enough.

LIVING A DRONE

When the sun's gone down, four birds, can't tell what
they are in the dark, play hopscotch in the chalk
squares on the sidewalk and they tweet the same
rhyme the children sing and the same cat who was
with the children earlier is watching these four birds
but no way is postured to pounce, rather is on its
back, feet in the air counting on its toes all the stars
out for the night when all of a sudden each bird grabs
a paw and together all five fly straight up in the air,
no sign of cat struggle whatsoever as the five of them
canvas the neighborhood, see and hear things even
more unbelievable than themselves.

V for WINGS

Man who's been manning the satellite reports he
hears geese sounding below like traffic on the New
Jersey Turnpike below them, communicable code he
hopes some teen idol sci geek is getting down with
digits as well as the geese's formations, some icon-
ic Vs, some like standard checkmarks, there was
that time a question mark, and some, cautions to
the wind, free sails when they're not geese at all but
broken-string kites and scratch paper airplanes and
origami blue loons whose honks when heard worldly,
signal it's time to be geese again for less than a mile
up ahead by earth's checkerboard standards, fans in
the thousands gather ovally in stadii, honk for their
favorite team's victory, only to be eclipsed by the re-
turning touchdowns of wings.

COMRADES IN ARMS, ETC.

I was talking with this fellow the other day down at
the diner, we were having a nice cup of coffee at the
counter and he told me after I asked him to pass the
sugar that he had two left feet and how he couldn't
drive a stick shift or hop around or he'd fall down and
he had to ride his bicycle sidesaddle and a bunch of
other stuff I pretended to hear and then he slipped
his sandals off and I'll be damned, all ten toes and
two arches going in the same direction and clumsy
me, I blamed it on my surprise when I spilt my coffee
and the counter creamer on the both of us and then's
when he suggested, and I obliged, to remove my
gloves and show him what he'd suspected all along,
my two right hands and a couple of months later after
each of us got our security deposits back, he moved
out of his handicapped apartment and I moved out of
mine and now we're practically joined at the hip in a
house just like yours.

GETTING HIGH

Terry falls for a tree and spends every waking hour in it, not to mention sleeping since he's found what he calls its most comfortable crotch and he's learning to walk out on its limbs, farther and farther each time and he knows how much give's in each one and what's really scary is he's begun licking its bark and sucking its sap, not so much as it would deprive the tree of the nourishment it needs, and those of us walking under it while Terry's in it never hear the two of them talking to each other so the voices we do hear must be coming from leaves and they're always talking at the same time, complaining one can't get a word in and oh, Terry has shed his shirt and dungarees but keeps his socks and boxers on, ironic he still gets cold feet and his skin has darkened a bit from exposure but his hair has gone long and blonde and he's begun to look a little like a tree himself, a tree in its teens, aspen perhaps who wonders if or when he will ever grow out of it and those of us who've had crushes on weeds and the occasional toad stool assure him he will but it's on him to take the first step.

NAME CHANGE GAME

He always liked the name Margie so he took it when his sister switched hers to Brian. He wrote it proudly on his T-shirt, across his ball cap. He often shouted it letter by letter from the patio while tending the grill. Everyday when he got his mail, he said to the mailman, hey, it's me, Margie and everyday the mailman zeroed in for his kiss. Brian wanted some action for herself and started making time with any tradesman who came by wearing his name stitched across his heart. Then one Tuesday after Margie and Brian woke up, they found the house had relocated itself to Fredericka Street with the front door now facing the backyard. Brian packed up and left and only a handyman knew where she went. Margie stayed put because he got hooked on grilling out front where the whole neighborhood could now watch him and catch a whiff of his shish kabobs and the house itself was taken in by this name change game, so much so it gave up Cookie Cutter for Totally Electric.

CORONATION

Eddie was across town, making his way home one night in a downpour when he knocked on a door and asked whoever answered for directions, saying he got turned around somehow in the dark and not only did he get directions but an umbrella as well and Eddie got away with this little maneuver umpteen times over the course of the evening all because of that damn smile and those warm eyes, so now he's home with twenty-two umbrellas and the next time it rains, he sets up an umbrella stand inside the lobby of town's tallest building and charges exorbitant prices during cloudbursts and repeats everything you've just heard multiple times and makes enough money, can you believe it, for a down payment on a modest re-do mid-Century Modern in Palm Springs, California that his two fathers had been dreaming about forever and Eddie ends up getting his own room with a cute little patio outside the sliding glass doors and the biggest umbrella he'd ever seen growing out of a table on which he now folds his hands and reigns over the tenth green as Edward.

SIX

Just when is any time soon?
I'll be waiting on the platform.

FUNNY WEATHER

The iceberg showed up three or four in the morning
at the last exit off the turnpike and gradually made
its way into town down Main, slipping and sliding
past dogs and cars left out overnight and dogs left in
cars overnight and later that afternoon, say between
three and four, time took on a new face, I mean,
shoppers were taking more of it talking to one an-
other, more of it gazing at unbeatables in the shop
windows, more of it watching the iceberg become for
one moment what appeared to be a cube, although
one gazer saw what he thought was a naked lady like
he'd once found floating in his highball, even the
parking meters were taking their time ticking away
time while beatcops' twirling blackjacks were un-
dercutting the second hand on the courthouse clock
and then, then, as if the end of an era, more likely
just quitting time, no iceberg, no iceberg anywhere
and each cop now walked a dog and let those still
in cars, out, and shoppers everywhere rushed home
with their treasures and just so you know, Main re-
mains a bit slick and frosty even in July.

DOUBLE MAJOR

After high school Marvel double-majored in cosmol-
ogy and cosmetology at the local community college
and now every night like clockwork she gathers to-
gether her paraphernalia and makes up stars. She's
even won awards. Her husband says she's bitten off
more than she can chew but one thing's sure, she
keeps them looking younger by millennia and some
scholars out there as well as in here say she's chang-
ing the faces of astrology and astronomy.

PHALLIC SENTIMENTS

Clarence confessed to me if he could do it all over again he'd have been a candlestick maker and I tell him there's still time, you're young and wick and wax are still reasonable but he's had his urology practice for nearly forty years now and he knows half the town by their penises alone and then he remembered how much fun and how much money he made summers with his popsicle stand at the end of his driveway and I informed him that sticks are a dime a dozen anymore and then he asks me how I've become so content waving a baton in the air twice a week in front of instruments and thousands of people and I tell him the baton itself is content and it's leading me, it's like a candle, a popsicle, a penis all rolled into one and I go places where I can't go without it but right now, I'm going to stick some kabobs on the grill. You want one?

NO SHOW OR TELL

Rita's ditched her cancer sticks for wooden sticks she
walks with every other hour or when the pitch goes
high along the black macadam or sandy sidewalk
with its many cracks which yesterday she took toward
town and found a burning butt she knew still held at
least two drags which she forewent and then her foot
got stuck to a wad of gum that just so happened to ex-
actly patch the hole beneath her arch, the gum, pink
bubblegum, same brand she used to blow big bubbles
and fill with smoke, Tareyton smoke while half the
block would gather 'round and urge her on to fill the
sky up and she'd smoke half a pack to fill one bub-
blegum cigar's whole bubblesworth whose secret for
success hides out inside what's left of lung.

PILGRIMS

Johnny can lift more than his weight, so proved when he carried his Mary over the threshold. It wasn't that long after the honeymoon. He admits now he should have used a dolly. Since then Mary's taken off a few; he's put on more. One evening after something resembling Thanksgiving, Johnny carried her out to their car and put her in. They drove up to the old high school overlook and parked. The car rocked. The rocks rocked. Something of a 4 on the Richter Scale. Johnny and Mary are now living in that car. It was and always will be their Plymouth.

ABUZZ

Sue was easy around bees, like a relative, and the neighbors noticed how she often ended her words with a kind of zzzing sound so when a grease fire from Bob's barbeque swept a crop of backyards last Saturday, Sue lost no time in wrestling the hornet's nest from the dogwood and flighting it to the bird-bath out front without so much as a sting and while the bees swarmed all around her, she was having a conversation with them and later that afternoon, she carried out some balls of yarn, cut them into strands and snagged them to the bees' stingers. Needless to say this took awhile and neighbors did-n't pay her much mind until about four in the after-noon when the bees started streaming strands all up and down her arms and around her neck and torso and Sue knew to hold very still, as still as still can get, not for fear of getting stung but to make sure this latest in beekeeping fashion would fit perfectly as she somehow knew the bees would have it no oth-er way and when they were done and Sue looked like a queen in her new yellow turtleneck, all of the out-of-work folks in the neighborhood began to come by everyday to help out with the little odd jobs that were beneath her around the house and garden.

FEAT

Clarissa's and her family's house went in the flood,
wishy-washed along with neighbors' down the river
to the ocean, bypassing the two bays but her little
dollhouse she clung to all the way to the shelter on
the hilltop and when danger was reported to have
passed, she returned to the flats with her family and
other families with little daughters clutching their
doll houses and remarkably, after days, variety packs
of flowers were seen popping up and light sprinkles
had washed most of the mud off the green growth
and each family returned to its lot where the cellar
had filled up with muck and it was there in that muck
Clarissa dug a hole with her little bare hands and
planted her little dollhouse with all of its contents
still inside and camped out on top of it with her fam-
ily and when morning came around, a great big house
had astonishingly sprung up and everyone found
themselves inside it astonishingly and when they
looked out of its windows up and down the street,
more great big houses with neighbors looking out of
their windows and waving with smiles on their fac-
es and big eyes like those big eyes you'd sometimes
see in garage sale paintings but no one was running
around outside because no one could get outside as
the windows in these great big houses didn't open
nor the doors so what else but mass panic through-
out the neighborhood until Clarissa remembered
that the roof lifted off and could be set down right
there in the backyard and once she performed her
little feat, big actually, with help from the same
little gophers who'd worked so hard all night,

in reality the pool boy and his brothers, all the
neighbors up and down the street followed suit and
weeks later NOAA wanted to name a tornado af-
ter her but she refused to accept because she could
also put the roof back on.

AT THE LAST MINUTE

When I was this kid in grade school I asked Junie who
sat cattycorner to me where she got the purple fruit
I saw in her lunch pail and she said it came with the
lunch pail and that she was going to keep it until her
mother returned the lunch pail because of the purple
fruit that came in it and when I suggested we just go
ahead and eat the purple fruit, she suggested I ask my
own mother to buy me a lunch pail with a purple fruit
in it and I told her I have no mother or even a moth-
er-in-law and Junie said I could have hers if that was
okay and I said I'd have to ask my dad as I did have a
dad, then Junie said she wasn't sure what a dad was
because apparently she didn't have one of those so
we decided at the last minute to eat the purple fruit
after all and I split it nicely down the middle with my
pocket knife and her lunch pail, well, of course we
had to flatten it now the purple fruit was gone and so
we did, taking turns with the little sledge hammer she
carried in her book bag.

SETTING THINGS RIGHT ON A FRIDAY NIGHT

I was going for a walk in the almost dark when head-
lights from behind lit up a porcupine a few feet ahead
and I didn't mind shooting the breeze with her but
not before we left the macadam for the short grass
and the porcupine told me right off she was attracted
to my dark gray suede shoes, same color and texture
she said as the hide beneath all her quills and no,
neither she nor any other porcupine she knew could
catapult them into my skin and she instructed me
how to stroke her, she so liked being stroked and
how almost impossible it was to find anyone who'd
do it and when I did it, the quills tickled us both and
she asked if she could run her paws over my shoes
and I said, sure, why not, what could it hurt and I
thought she might be falling in love, then she told
me her twin boys had been struck by a pickup and
succumbed in the tangle of witch hazel beyond the
U-curve so what else could I do but give them to her,
leaving me to make it home barefoot in the fine light
of a new moon.

CROSSING WIRES

Two phone booths of the red and silver variety with uncooperative folding doors stand side by side on the corner. I go in the one on the left, drop in my dime and dial. I hear a ring but no one answers. I get my dime back and try again. Just as the phone rings again, a man goes in the phone booth next to mine and picks up the receiver. Before he drops in his dime, he hears me say, Ron, is that you? No, I hear him say back through the glass, this is Rob. Sorry, I say and hang up. So does Rob. Third time's a charm so I dig for another dime and seconds before I drop it in the slot, the phone rings in my booth. I pick up. It's Rob from the booth next door. Sorry, we both say together and hang up. I give up and walk on to the next corner where a lone booth stands next to the newspaper dispenser. I drop in a dime and take out today's. I take it with me into the lone booth and discover my pockets are now empty. The phone rings and I pick up. The voice on the other end says, hello. I say, Ron, is that you, is that really you? Ron says, of course it's me, who'd you think it would be? Rob? You didn't see what happened to him in the paper?

YELLOW RIBBON 'ROUND

It was in all the papers. One winter night someone or something emptied out the pound, the one on Prospect Street. Dogs and cats alike, gone. The place reportedly smelled like roses after. Folks began calling the police, their representatives' local offices, saying they had found a dog, a cat tied to their mailbox posts or to a shrub near their front doors, each with a yellow ribbon loosely in a bow around its neck. What's more, what's most, it was reported, is each receiver was delighted, the cat or dog exactly what he or she had wanted and it showed up at precisely the right time but there seemed to be a catch. The ribbon around the animal's neck would not come off no matter what was tried, could not be loosened, could not be cut even with the sharpest scissors but it always stayed clean and bright. It was as much a pet part as a tail or paw or whiskers. What is even more impressive is these dogs and cats are still alive thirty-six years later. We got our beagle when I was just a kid and my neighbor down the street, her tiger when she was ten. Our plumber also got a pet, mongrel that it was, and found a way to get its ribbon off. He heated it with his blowtorch and stretched it and as you'd guess, poor thing immediately caught fire and that was that. Oh, did I tell you where my step sis got the ribbon?

LEND

Last time Roger was asked to lend a hand to some-body, he didn't get it back for a month and when he finally did, he didn't recognize it as his as it had what looked like new flesh and was decidedly quiet-er, didn't crack and pop when he curled up its fin-gers and the fist it made was more gavel than sledge and he found himself waving a lot more now and to practically everybody, continuing to wave even after everybody'd stopped as if the hand he now held had a will of its own or had a lot of make-up waving to do or maybe the borrower had put a chip in it con-trolled through an app from a cell phone so Roger sought out the borrower and told him he'd like his original hand back and the borrower agreed, hand-ing him, along with his hand, Roger's old transistor radio from the sixties which he'd once glued to his one good ear, one he will never again lend to any-body no matter what time it is.

ALIGNMENTS

Quincy was asked to speak in front of a bunch of Rotarians last Thursday night and after he was introduced, he walked up on stage and sat down at a piano left over from Wednesday night's ladies' auxiliary sing-a-long but Quincy didn't know how to play a piano so he got up off the bench to face a thunderous applause and of course the correct and polite thing to do was take a bow so he did and the applause grew even louder and he wasn't sure if they were applauding because he didn't play anything or they just really admired the arch in his back while he was sitting on the bench, the most beautiful alignment of vertebrae anyone'd ever seen so he decided to sit back down on the bench and the room grew quiet and Quincy didn't know what to do for an encore so he just sat there for a few minutes cracking his knuckles, the audience holding its breath when he noticed his fingernails were in pretty bad shape, long and chipped with cuticles askew so he chewed on the few that were out of line with the others and when he was done chewing and spitting, he rose from the bench to an even greater applause, more cyclonic than thunderous and when he got home which took no time at all walking on clouds, Quincy found his answering machine filled with requests, all shaky car owners asking if he could do his magic on wheels.

GRAND THEFT

Doe browses the underbrush behind Quick Mart, raises her head, sees a man climb into a Ram and become a wild wooly beast with bright eyes, cloven feet. Doe watches a woman with hair that does not move and big black adjustable eyes step into a sun-streaked Cougar with its hat off, slink into the stampede of traffic. When a cherry-red Impala with turquoise-tinted windshield, chrome-plated grill and white sidewall tires idles at an angle by the ice machine, doe does, doe does what, doe does what she knows, doe does what she knows she has to do, even if it means breaking the law.

DEAR ENVELOPE,

Ever since I first laid eyes on you, then held you in
my hands, I've had the urge to part you at the seams.
I simply want to know your shape, you know, before
the folds and glue.

I'd like to lick you too, if you will promise not
to bite my tongue. On second thought, with all the
poison being posted, I'll use my finger and a drop of
water.

How long have you been wearing underwear, es-
pecially security blue weave? To snoop, I'll have to
steam you open. I liked you best when I could see
right through you to a claim of love, an insincere
apology, an order to pay up or else. Almost forgot,
rejection slips!

Maybe you could use a rest. Or some refinement,
a return to stamps engraved with precious inks. And
penmanship direct from someone's fountain pen
with such signature finesse, all know who you're
from! And ending with some hot wax and seal.

For all I know you could be happy with your new
self-seal, the rapid sorting, coded bars. Vulgar post-
cards you eschewed and email never will deliver
your occasional perfume, your linen skin, my heavy
breathing as I open what's inside. No matter what, I
know we'll always be in touch.

C.R.S.

ABOUT THE AUTHOR

Charles Springer has degrees in anthropology and is an award-winning painter. A Pushcart Prize, Sonder Press Best Small Fictions, and Best of the Net nominee, he is widely published in print and online. His first collection of poems entitled *Juice* was published by Regal House Publishing. Charles writes from Pennsylvania.